THE CHRISTMAS LEGACY

A POEM

ADAPTED BY FLAVIA AND LISA WEEDN
ILLUSTRATED BY FLAVIA WEEDN

Cedco Publishing • San Rafael, California

Our family has cherished this poem since it was originally written in 1943, during World War II. It was a special gift from 1st Lt. Jack Money to his niece, Judy, on her very first Christmas.

These simple words remind us that life is a gift to be cherished, and that children bring into our hearts the most beautiful offering of all . . . and that is love.

Jack would be very proud, as we are, to share this legacy with all children.

Merry Christmas.

The lights

are dim,

but atop

the tree

a star is

shining bright

for

in spite

of closing

darkness

it's

Christmas

Eve

tonight.

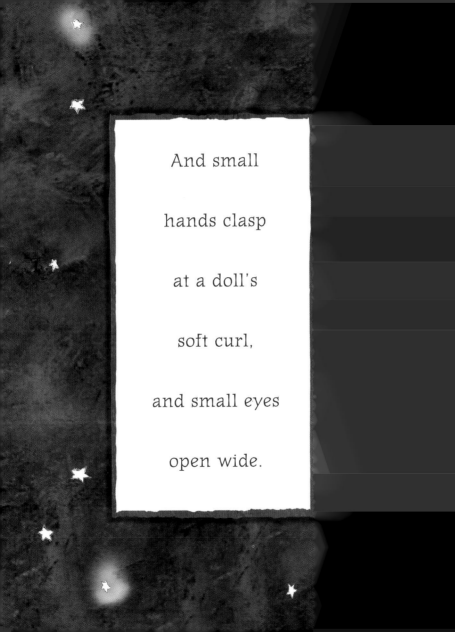

And small

hands clasp

at a doll's

soft curl,

and small eyes

open wide.

And a small

heart thrills

with happiness

at the presents

side by side.

But dear

little one,

the things

you have

are more

than

those

you see.

The real

gifts

at this

Christmastime

are not

placed

on the

tree.

A family

close

in love

and joy,

the

care

that they

can

give,

the promise you

shall always

have,

this country

in which to live.

Each may have

his presents,

but yours are

more precious,

dear . . .

for you

give love

and hope

anew

and you

give it

by just

being

here.